LEAVE HORATIO ALONE

Eleanor Clymer

LEAVE HORATIO ALONE

ILLUSTRATED BY

Robert Quackenbush

ATHENEUM   *1974*   NEW YORK

To Georgia/E.C.

To Piet Robert/R.Q.

HORATIO was a cat. He was a large, middle-aged, striped cat, and he lived with a lady named Mrs. Casey, in a brick house on a city street.

He was not the only one who lived there. There was also a puppy named Sam, a rabbit, a pigeon and two kittens, one yellow, the other black. Mrs. Casey had taken them in because they had no other place to live.

Horatio liked everything to be quiet and orderly. The other animals were just the opposite.

The pigeon flopped around dropping bird seed.

The rabbit left bits of carrot and lettuce all over the floor. He liked to pop out from under the sofa.

The puppy chewed things and barked.

The kittens ran all over the house, knocked over lamps, and jumped on Horatio's tail. They seemed to think it was there for them to play with.

It wasn't so bad in summer. Then Horatio could go out and sit under a bush. But now it was winter, too cold to stay out.

Mrs. Casey was very patient. She tidied up the house. And she said, "Leave Horatio alone. He's older than you, and he doesn't feel like playing."

But one day Mrs. Casey had to go away. She packed a few things in a small suitcase and put on her good black coat and her red hat.

Horatio did not like it when she went out. It was bad enough when she put on her old things to go to market. But when he saw the red hat and the suitcase, he knew this was different. He jumped into the suitcase and sat in it.

Mrs. Casey gently lifted him out.

"No, Horatio," she said. "I must go to see my daughter. She needs me to help her with the twins. I'll be back tomorrow. Michael and Betsy will come to take care of you."

Michael and Betsy were two children who lived next door.

Horatio followed Mrs. Casey to the door, but she closed it before he could get out. He lay down on the doormat.

Sam, the puppy, found him there. He rushed at Horatio and barked. He wanted Horatio to run away so he could chase him.

Horatio got up and went to his favorite chair. He curled up with his paws and tail tucked in. The puppy could not reach him there. But the kittens could. They climbed up the back of the chair and jumped on him.

Horatio shook them off and went upstairs. In Mrs. Casey's bedroom there was a tall closet. He got on the top of that. It was too tall for the kittens to climb. There he spent the afternoon.

At suppertime, Michael and Betsy came to feed the animals. Their mother came to help.

Horatio did not like her way of doing things. She was in a great hurry. She opened cans and poked the food out. She did not bother to mix it properly with bits of leftover good things, as Mrs. Casey did. She poured out some milk and put out bird seed and rabbit food and lettuce leaves.

The children wanted to stay and play, but their mother said, "No. We must hurry home and get supper for Daddy."

Horatio tried to eat his supper, but it didn't taste right. He scratched the floor with his paw and walked away. He went to the back door intending to go out, but the lady had not left it open for him. So he went back to the closet.

The evening was long and dull. Downstairs he could hear Sam and the kittens running about. Once he heard a crash. Something had been knocked over.

In the morning, Michael and Betsy came back, with their mother. She opened some more cans and fed the animals. But she did not put Horatio's food in his special bowl.

Horatio ate a little. He hunched himself up on the top of the refrigerator, looking miserable.

Michael asked, "Mother, may we stay here and play?"

"All right," their mother said. "Just a little while. I'll come back for you in half an hour." And she left.

Michael played ball with Sam. Betsy tied a string to a piece of paper for the kittens to chase. She tried to get Horatio to play too, but he wouldn't.

He didn't like this at all. He went back to the closet. It was selfish of Mrs. Casey to go off like this. Did she plan to come back at all? Horatio couldn't remember. He did not enjoy spending all his time on the closet.

When the children's mother came back for them, he jumped down and went to the door.

"Come along," the lady said, holding the door open.

"Don't let Horatio out!" Michael called. But it was too late. Horatio had scooted outside.

"Come back, Horatio!" they called. But he pretended not to hear. He ran along the street and hid behind a trash can. The children called and called, but he did not answer. They wanted to look for him, but their mother said, "He'll come back. Don't worry. We have to go to the store now."

Horatio trotted along the street, looking carefully for dogs and sniffing at a number of garbage cans. One of them smelled of fish, but the top was on tight.

It was getting colder. Horatio could feel it in his feet and his nose. The rest of him was warm, since it was covered with fur. But he was getting hungry. He wished he had eaten more breakfast.

And now something began to fall from the sky. Something white and wet. It was snowing. The flakes drifted down and stuck to Horatio's fur. He trotted around a corner. He looked at one house after another. Every door was closed.

At last he came to a house that had a little porch. He ran up the steps and crouched there. At least it wasn't so wet. But it *was* cold. Horatio shivered.

Was anybody at home? Horatio decided to find out. He scratched at the door and called, "Meow!" as loudly as he could. The door opened. There was a girl, somewhat bigger than Betsy.

"Oh, look!" she called. "A cat! Come in, pussycat."

Horatio walked in, and she closed the door. "Ellen! Baby!" she called. "Come and see."

Two more children came running down the stairs. They sat down on the floor, and the biggest one pulled Horatio into her lap. The others patted his fur.

"Look, Maryjane," said the one called Ellen, "he's wet."

She ran and got a towel and began to rub him with it. But she rubbed the wrong way.

The smallest one tried to put her finger in Horatio's eye.

"No, Baby, don't do that," said Maryjane. "He might scratch."

"I certainly might," thought Horatio.

"Let's see if he's hungry," said Ellen. She picked Horatio up and carried him to the kitchen.

"I can walk," Horatio muttered, but she didn't understand him.

He was big and heavy, and she was holding him by the middle with his legs hanging down.

She put him down, and Maryjane poured some milk into a saucer. Horatio drank it and purred. It was his way of saying, "Thank you, that was good, is there anything more?"

"Oh, he's purring," said Ellen. "He likes us."

"That's what you think," Horatio muttered.

Maryjane looked in the refrigerator and found a piece of chicken. She gave it to Horatio, and he chewed it. It had salt and pepper on it, but it was better than nothing.

While he ate, the baby pulled his tail.

"Don't do that," said Maryjane.

The baby stopped pulling his tail and pulled his whiskers.

Horatio took the chicken in his teeth and crawled behind the refrigerator. It was pretty dusty back there, but at least he was able to finish eating. Then he came out. His whiskers were covered with spiderwebs. He was just about to wash his face when Ellen said, "Let's take him upstairs."

They carried him up and took turns holding him. The baby swatted him with a sticky hand.

"Meow!" said Horatio.

He thought someone might say, "Leave Horatio alone." But there didn't seem to be any big people in this house.

Ellen said, "I wonder if Mother will let us keep this cat. We'll ask her when she comes home."

Maryjane said, "Let's dress him up." They found some dolls' clothes and began to dress Horatio. One girl squeezed his forepaws into a doll's dress. The other tied a bonnet under his chin.

They held him up in front of the mirror so he could see himself.

Horatio was very angry. He jumped out of the girls' arms and ran down the stairs and hid behind the sofa.

The baby followed him, calling. "Come back, pussycat!"

Horatio ran to the front door. It was not latched. He put his paw around the edge, and it swung open. He ran out.

"I'd better go home," he thought. "Even if Mrs. Casey isn't there, Michael and Betsy are better than this lot."

He ran along the street, leaving little round paw prints in the snow. It was hard to run with the doll's dress on, so he sat down and tore at it with his teeth. At last it came off. Then he clawed at the bonnet till it came off too. He was just starting off again when he heard, "Come here, pussycat!"

It was Baby. She was coming after him.

Horatio ran to the corner. Baby came too. If only he could remember where his house was. He turned the corner.

Oh! Now he knew where he was. There was the house, halfway down the block. Horatio ran to it. He bounded up the steps and scratched at the door.

"Meow!" he called in his loudest voice.

The door flew open. There were Michael and Betsy, and right behind them was Mrs. Casey.

"Horatio! Where have you been?" she cried, picking him up. "And who is this with you?"

There was Baby, trotting along, rather wet with snow, and calling out, "Pussycat!"

Mrs. Casey put Horatio down and picked up the baby.

"You poor little thing!" she said. "All wet and cold. Horatio, where did you find her?"

"Find her indeed," thought Horatio. "She found me. And I hope you're not going to keep her. Kittens are one thing, but a baby is impossible."

But Mrs. Casey had no idea of keeping Baby. "I wonder where she lives," she said.

"Oh, I know her," said Betsy. "She's Ellen's and Maryjane's sister. She lives around the corner."

"Pussycat!" said Baby, reaching for Horatio.

Mrs. Casey put a blanket around Baby. She telephoned Baby's mother. Then she sat on the sofa in front of the fire, with Baby on her lap. Horatio had to sit on the sofa too, so Baby could pat him. It was the only way to keep her quiet.

A few minutes later, Baby's mother rushed in. She snatched Baby and kissed her ever so many times.

"Those naughty girls," she said, "not to watch their sister. How did you find her?"

"Horatio brought her home," said Mrs. Casey.

"What a wonderful cat!" said Baby's mother. "He's the smartest cat I ever saw. Say good-by to the pussycat, Baby."

Baby didn't want to say good-by. As her mother carried her to the door, she cried, "Take pussycat home!"

"The pussycat lives here," said Baby's mother. "We'll come back and see him soon."

"I hope not," growled Horatio.

At last the door was closed.

"Thank goodness," Horatio thought, rubbing against Mrs. Casey's ankles.

"Poor Horatio, you must be hungry," she said. "Come and have some supper."

Much later, Horatio sat in Mrs. Casey's lap. He was dry and warm, and his stomach was full of tuna fish, which he liked even better than liver.

Michael and Betsy were sitting on the rug, playing with the kittens. Betsy had a ball tied to a string. The kittens batted it back and forth.

Horatio watched them sleepily.

"Really, these children are not so bad," he thought. "At least they don't dress me up in ridiculous clothes. And the kittens and Sam aren't so bad either. After all, they're still young. I was young once too."

Suddenly he remembered what it was like to be young. You wanted to play all the time.

He jumped down from Mrs. Casey's lap. He walked over to the ball and batted it with his paw. Then he pounced on it. The kittens leaped on Horatio and they all rolled over, pretending to bite each other.

"Look, Mrs. Casey!" said Betsy. "Horatio is playing!"